DISNEY

Winnie the Pooh

5-Minute Stories

DISNEY PRESS
Los Angeles • New York

Contents

Be Patient, Pooh

One morning, Winnie the Pooh woke up thinking about cake, presents, and balloons. It's not every day that a bear wakes up thinking of those things. But this day was Pooh's birthday, and his friends were throwing him a party.

A birthday party for me, Pooh thought excitedly. *I can't wait!*

He leapt out of bed and looked at his clock. "Is it time for my birthday party yet?" he asked. The clock's little hand pointed at the eight, and the big hand pointed at the twelve. *Breakfast time,* thought Pooh. *That's always a good time.*

He went to the kitchen and pulled out three pots of honey. "By the time I've finished these, it'll be almost time for my party," he said.

But when he'd licked the last drop of honey from the bottom of the third pot, it still wasn't time for his party.

Next Pooh did some exercises in his bedroom. Once he had finished a round of them, he did the exercises again. When he was done, it still wasn't time for his party.

"I'd better go to Rabbit's house to see how the party is coming along," Pooh said to himself as he hurried to his friend's home.

3

When Pooh arrived at Rabbit's, he knocked loudly on his friend's door. "How's the party coming?" Pooh asked.

"Everything is fine," Rabbit said as he opened the door. "The party will be ready at dinnertime."

"Can I see my cake?" Pooh asked. He tried to look around Rabbit.

"Not yet," Rabbit said, blocking Pooh's view. "You have to wait until dinnertime!"

Pooh sighed. It wasn't anywhere near dinnertime yet. And the morning had been longer than any other morning he could remember. He sat down on his favorite rock near the stream. He watched the bubbly water racing past. "The water must be rushing to a birthday party," Pooh said.

Maybe having a little company would help pass the time, thought Pooh.

He knocked at Piglet's door, and he could hear the sound of paper rustling inside. "Are you wrapping my present, Piglet?" Pooh asked.

"Don't come in yet!" Piglet cried. He finished tying a purple ribbon around Pooh's present and hid it in the closet.

"You can come in now," he called to Pooh.

"Can I see my present, Piglet? What do you think we'll do at the party, Piglet? Do you think Rabbit will put pink roses on my cake? How much longer do you think it'll be, Piglet?" Pooh asked breathlessly.

He settled in Piglet's comfy chair. "It is nice to have company to talk to about all these things," Pooh said. "It helps pass the time in a friendly way. Doesn't it?"

Piglet was trying to decide which question to answer first when Tigger and Roo knocked at the door.

"Lunchtime!" Tigger cried as he and Roo bounced in.

Piglet looked at his clock. The big hand and the little hand were both pointing to twelve.

"Lunchtime," said Pooh thoughtfully. "That's a lot closer to dinnertime than breakfast time is, isn't it?"

"It's right NOW," Tigger said impatiently.

"Lunchtime is one of my favorite times of day," said Pooh. He helped Piglet, Tigger, and Roo set the table.

As Pooh licked his last pot of honey clean, he sighed happily. "This is almost like a party right now."

"Oh, no," said Tigger, "a party has streamers and noisemakers and fancy hats and ice cream and . . ."

Pooh thought about streamers and noisemakers and fancy hats and ice cream and cake and presents and balloons. . . . "Is it almost time for the party?" he asked.

"Oh, d-dear, I hope not," Piglet said. "I promised to help Rabbit decorate."

"Me too," said Tigger.

"Me too, too," added Roo.

Piglet, Tigger, and Roo hurried off to Rabbit's house.

While Pooh waited, he decided to wash Piglet's lunch dishes. *By the time I finish these, it will be time for my party,* he thought. But when he had dried the last drop of water from the last dish, it was still not time for his party.

"Waiting is hard," sighed Pooh. "Maybe I should ask Christopher Robin if he knows something about it."

When Pooh arrived at Christopher Robin's house, he asked his friend his question. "Why does it take so long for it to be time for a party?"

"It just seems long, Pooh," Christopher Robin said. "When you have to wait, the best thing to do is something you really like."

"What do bears like to do?" asked Pooh, hoping Christopher Robin could remind him.

"Well, I'm reading this great story about a pirate bear who's looking for buried treasure," Christopher Robin said. "Would you like me to read it to you?"

"Yes, please," Pooh said happily.

The two friends snuggled together under a shady tree, and Christopher Robin began to read. Pooh forgot all about cake, presents, and balloons. He closed his eyes and saw tall ships, rolling waves, and buried treasure. They were almost to the end when Christopher Robin checked his watch.

The little hand pointed at the five, and the big hand pointed at twelve. "Dinnertime!" he said to Pooh.

"You mean it's time for my party ALREADY?" Pooh cried.

Christopher Robin took Pooh's present from its hiding place and headed toward Rabbit's house. "Come on, Pooh," he called.

"Cake and presents and balloons! It's time, it's time, it's time!" sang Pooh as they walked along together.

Pooh was the first one to reach the door. Rabbit swung it open and shouted, "Happy birthday!"

Inside, Pooh saw his beautiful birthday cake with pink roses, honey pots all wrapped in festive paper, lots of colorful balloons, and streamers. "Happy birthday, Pooh!" his friends all shouted. Everyone was there—Eeyore, Rabbit, Kanga, Roo, Owl, Tigger, and Piglet!

"Oh!" cried Pooh. "Party time is my favorite time ever!"

Then Pooh hugged his good friends Piglet and Christopher Robin.

"And thanks to you two," he whispered, "waiting was a lot of fun, too."

Roo's New Babysitter

"Roo, dear, your babysitter will be here soon," Kanga said.

"I don't want to be babysitted!" Roo cried.

"Now, Roo. Mama's just going out for a little shopping and dinner with Aunt Sadie," said Kanga. "You'll have fun with Pooh."

"But I want to go shopping with YOU!" Roo cried. "I'm really good at shopping. I can help."

"Yes, dear, I know," Kanga said. She was busy buttoning her coat and looking for her purse.

Roo found a large bag and began filling it with things. "Look at me shopping!" he cried. "I'd be such a big help!"

"Another time, dear," Kanga said.

"What other time?" asked Roo.

"Well, not this time," Kanga said. "Oh, look! Here comes Pooh now."

"Hello, Pooh," said Roo. "Look! I'm shopping!"

"Now, Pooh, don't let Roo get into any mischief while I'm gone."

"Oh, I won't let him get into anything," said Pooh cheerfully.

"Good-bye!" Roo and Pooh waved as they watched Kanga hop down the path and over the bridge. When she was out of sight, Roo's face dropped.

Pooh gave Roo a hug as they walked back inside. Then Pooh put Roo in his high chair.

"What you need to cheer you up is a nice snack," Pooh said. "How about some honey?"

"I like shopping," squeaked Roo. "I don't want a snack."

"Hmmmm, he doesn't want to eat," Pooh said. "Now what do I do?"

"You don't know how to babysit?" asked Roo.

"Of course I do," Pooh said. "All except the actual babysitting part."

"I'm good at babysitting," Roo said, perking up. "I'll tell you how."

"The first thing a babysitter does is play store," said Roo.

He showed Pooh how to set up the cash register and where to put all the toys and cans and bags.

When they were finished playing, Pooh sat down to rest.

"The next thing a babysitter does is climb!" Roo cried. "Let's see who can climb higher—you or me."

Pooh was beginning to think there was not much sitting involved in babysitting. He sighed. "Okay, let's find a good tree to climb."

The old apple tree in Roo's backyard was perfect. Roo jumped up, but he couldn't reach even the lowest branch.

"Babysitters always give a boost," he said.

"I see," Pooh replied.

Roo hopped from branch to branch. Pooh climbed up behind him.
"Mmmm," said Roo. "Look at those apples. Babysitters always pick
apples for dinner."

Pooh scrambled up to the highest branch. He picked four bright red apples and tucked them under his arm. Then he inched his way back down.

"Wow, Pooh," Roo cried. "You can climb with one arm!"

"Oops! I'm just that sort of—*OOF!*—babysitter!" Pooh shouted as he fell onto Roo's branch.

Together, they sat side by side, swinging their feet and eating their sweet apples.

"This is the best dinner ever!" Roo said happily.

"What do babysitters do after dinner?" Pooh asked.

"They give baths with lots of bubbles," Roo said.

Inside, Roo showed Pooh how babysitters pour a whole bottle of bubble solution into the bathwater.

"That seems like a lot," Pooh said.

"Just right," Roo said.

Roo took off his little shirt and hopped in. He disappeared under the bubbles.

29

"Where's Roo?" Pooh asked. He blew on the bubbles. But he couldn't see Roo anywhere. Pooh frantically swished his hands through the bubbles. Roo was nowhere to be found!

"Look at me jumping," squeaked a little voice. Pooh could hear Roo!

"There you are!" Pooh cried as he walked into Roo's bedroom.

Roo was all bubbly and wet. He jumped up and down on his bed.

Pooh chased the little kangaroo with a towel. When he finally caught him, Pooh dried him off. "It's time to take your strengthening medicine," Pooh said sternly.

"I don't want it," said Roo. He folded his arms across his chest and stuck out his chin.

"Oh, well," Pooh sighed as he slumped into a chair. "Why don't you give me a spoonful? I'm not feeling so well. I think I could use it."

"Now, Pooh, dear, here's your medicine," Roo said in a grown-up voice. He fed Pooh a spoonful of medicine.

"Ahhh! Much better," Pooh sighed. "Thank you, Roo. You are a good babysitter."

"I'm babysitting!" Roo sang happily.

Just then, Kanga opened the door. She saw Roo and Pooh snuggled together in the chair.

"Mama! Look at me!" Roo shouted. "I'm babysitting Pooh!"

"Of course you are, dear," Kanga said with a smile.

The Sleepover

"Comfortable, Piglet?" Pooh asked. He was tucking his friend into a dresser drawer that had been made into a bed just the right size for Piglet.

"Oh, yes, Pooh. Thank you ever so much," Piglet replied.

The two friends were having a best-friend sleepover, which, as far as they could tell, had to involve sleeping *over* something.

"I suppose you could say that I'm sleeping *over* the other dresser drawer," said Piglet.

Pooh nodded. He looked around his house. "Now, I wonder what I should sleep over?"

Piglet looked around, too. But there seemed to be just one place that was well suited for Pooh: his own bed. So, in the end, that's what Pooh decided to sleep over.

"Well, good night, Piglet," said Pooh. He blew out the candle and climbed into bed.

"Good night, Pooh Bear," Piglet replied.

Piglet lay in the darkness of Pooh's room, comfortable in his drawer. What a wonderful best-friend sleepover it had been so far, he thought.

First Piglet and Pooh had enjoyed a before-bedtime snack.

Next they had put on their pajamas.

Then they had made up a bedtime story together.

Of course, it was always fun spending time with Pooh. Although there was something about being at Pooh's house at bedtime that was so . . . so . . . *different* from being at Piglet's own house at bedtime.

As he lay there in the dresser drawer with his eyes wide open, it occurred to Piglet that the darkness at Pooh's house was much, much darker than it was at his own house. So Piglet rolled over and pulled up the covers. Then he closed his eyes tight and tried to fall asleep. But nothing happened.

Piglet opened one eye and peeked out into the darkness. That's when he noticed that it was very, very quiet in Pooh's room. Much quieter than the quiet in Piglet's own room at night.

In particular, the quiet that was coming from the direction of Pooh's bed, where Piglet's best friend was fast asleep while Piglet lay wide-awake—that was the quietest quiet of all.

"Pooh?" Piglet whispered. "Pooh Bear?" he called out, a little louder this time. He didn't want to wake up Pooh. Then Piglet wondered if perhaps Pooh was awake but had just not heard him. Still, there was no answer.

Piglet tried his best again to fall asleep.

Then he heard a soft, low rumbling. It was curiously similar to the sound of a sleeping bear snoring. As Piglet listened, the sound grew louder . . . and louder . . . and then softer and softer . . . and then louder and louder . . . over and over again! Was it the sound of an approaching heffalump? Piglet wondered. The sound continued.

"Pooh! Oh, d-d-dear!" Piglet shouted, jumping
out of the drawer and running to Pooh's bedside. He
shook Pooh as he shouted, "Wake up! Wake up! Oh,
p-p-please, P-P-Pooh!"

"Hmm?" Pooh said drowsily, sitting up. He climbed out of bed and walked over to light a candle. When it was lit, he found Piglet hiding under the covers in Pooh's bed.

"Why, Piglet," said Pooh, "what's the matter?"

Piglet was trembling so much it was hard to get the words out. "It's that horrible n-n-noise, Pooh," he stammered.

Piglet listened for the noise so he could point it out, then realized he couldn't hear it.

"That's funny," said Piglet as he peeked out from under the covers. "The noise stopped as soon as you woke up, Pooh."

"Hmm," said Pooh. He shrugged. Then he yawned. "I guess that means we can go back to sleep."

Piglet wasn't so sure. He didn't want to hurt Pooh's feelings. But he didn't think he could fall asleep in Pooh's room.

"Pooh Bear," said Piglet timidly, "I don't mean to be a bad best friend. But do you think we might . . . well . . . have the rest of our best-friend sleepover some other night? I'm just not used to sleeping anywhere but my own house."

Pooh sat down on the bed and put his arm around Piglet. "I understand, Piglet," he said. "We can have the rest of our best-friend sleepover whenever you like."

Pooh helped Piglet gather his things, including his very own pillow.

Then, hand in hand, Pooh and Piglet began to
walk through the Hundred-Acre Wood. It was a short
stroll through the forest to Piglet's house. The stars
were still twinkling in the night sky when the two best
friends arrived.

"Here you are, Piglet," Pooh said as they entered.
"Home, sweet home."

Piglet was very glad to be at his own house.

"Oh, thank you, Pooh," he said. "Thank you so much for understanding and for walking me back. I suppose you'll need to get home to bed now?"

Pooh considered the question.

"That does sound like the thing to do," he said. "But first I might sit down for a little rest." Pooh noticed a comfortable-looking chair. "Just for a few minutes, of course."

While Piglet put away his things, Pooh sat down in the chair. It was even more comfortable than it looked. Pooh put up his feet. Then he decided to rest his eyes, just for a moment.

By the time Piglet came back, Pooh was fast asleep. He was even making a soft, low rumbling sound. But in the comfort of his own house, it did not strike Piglet as anything other than the sound of one sleeping bear snoring.

Piglet covered his best friend with a small blanket and slipped a pillow under his head. "Sweet dreams, Pooh Bear," he whispered.

Then Piglet climbed into his own bed and drifted off to sleep. It seemed that he and Pooh were having their best-friend sleepover, after all.

Eeyore's Good Day

The sun was only just reaching its highest point in the sky over the Hundred-Acre Wood. But already it had been a friend-filled day for Winnie the Pooh and Piglet. Early that morning, they had agreed it was a good day to visit all their friends.

First they had dropped in on Kanga and Roo, who were just finishing their breakfast.

"What a pleasant surprise!" Kanga had said. She had welcomed them inside and set two more places at the table. Pooh had already had a full breakfast. But the walk to Kanga and Roo's house had made Pooh and Piglet hungry!

Next Pooh and Piglet had stopped at Rabbit's house, just in time for a midmorning snack. Rabbit was happy to see his friends while he took a break from working on his garden.

And later that morning, they had dropped in to say hello at Owl's. He was just beginning to fix his lunch and invited Pooh and Piglet to join him.

"I'm not sure we can stay for lunch," Piglet said. "We have a few more friends to visit."

Pooh scratched his chin and rubbed his tummy, deep in thought. "Though I suppose that means we'd better keep up our strength!" he said at last, plopping down into one of Owl's chairs.

Now, as Pooh and Piglet made their way toward Eeyore's house, Pooh felt pleasantly full, while Piglet felt overstuffed. He hoped that Eeyore had no food to offer.

"Good afternoon, Eeyore!" Piglet called out as he and Pooh spotted their friend sitting in the sun.

"Oh, hello," Eeyore replied glumly. "What brings you out to my gloomy part of the Wood?"

Pooh looked up at the blue sky and bright sun. "It doesn't seem very gloomy to me," he said.

Eeyore turned his eyes skyward. "Hmm," he said flatly. "I suppose you're right."

"Is anything the matter, Eeyore?" Piglet asked.

Eeyore thought it over. "No," he said at last. "I suppose nothing is the matter today."

Pooh and Piglet looked at each other, puzzled. Neither was quite sure what to say. Nothing the matter? Usually Eeyore had at least one trouble to report—that his tail had fallen off, or his house had fallen down or been moved when he wasn't looking.

Eeyore lay down and sighed a heavy sigh. "I guess this is what some folks would call 'a good day.' I call it downright uncomfortable."

Pooh scratched his head. "Uncomfortable?" he said.

Eeyore nodded. "I'm not complaining," he said, "but 'nothing the matter' feels an awful lot like 'something the matter' to me."

Suddenly, Piglet had an idea. "Pardon me, Eeyore," he said. "I need to talk to Pooh for a second."

Piglet pulled Pooh aside and whispered in his ear so that Eeyore could not hear.

"Pooh Bear, I was wondering," Piglet began. "Do you think Eeyore would feel better if something *were* the matter?"

"I think that very well may be," Pooh whispered back.

"I was thinking if you and I were to make something the matter—just temporarily, of course—perhaps Eeyore would feel more like himself," Piglet suggested.

Pooh and Piglet decided they would ask Eeyore to come with them to visit Christopher Robin. They figured that would take his mind off his problems—or rather, his lack of problems.

But on the way back to Eeyore, Piglet stooped to examine a tiny ladybug on a flower. Pooh, who was walking right behind him, didn't see Piglet stop.

Pooh stumbled over poor Piglet and flew through the air toward Eeyore. At the very last moment, Eeyore stepped out of the way, and Pooh tumbled full-speed into Eeyore's house. Eeyore's house came crashing down to the ground.

"Don't worry, Eeyore," Piglet reassured him. "We'll rebuild it for you. Won't we, Pooh?"

"Yes, yes!" Pooh replied. And he and Piglet went right to work, putting the house back together as Eeyore looked on.

As Eeyore watched his friends rebuild his house, the smallest smile worked its way across his face. Was it because now there was something the matter, and that felt more natural to the gray donkey?

Or was it watching two good friends working hard to cheer up another that made Eeyore's spirits lift? Whatever the reason, all three friends agreed it had turned out to be a very good day indeed.

Tigger's Moving Day

One morning, Rabbit was having breakfast at Tigger's house. After they'd eaten, Tigger stood up and stretched. "Time for my morning bounce!" he cried.

Sproing! Sproing! Sproing!

"Look out!" Rabbit cried.

THUMP! Tigger bumped into one of his cupboards, and everything flew out of it. "Whoops. That happens every time!"

"Tigger, you don't have enough bouncing room in this little house of yours," Rabbit said.

PLUNK! A toy truck toppled off a nearby shelf and landed on Tigger's head. "Ouch!" he cried. "It's true. But what can I do?"

"We've got to find you a bigger house!" Rabbit declared. "That's all there is to it."

"But . . ." Tigger began.

"No buts," Rabbit said. "I'm going to organize our friends right away. Don't worry—we're going to find you the perfect new home."

Rabbit quickly gathered everyone. They spent the day looking for the right house for their friend. By the end of the day, the friends were excited about the big new house they had found for Tigger.

"It IS a bouncy house," Tigger said. "That's the kind of house Tiggers like best!" Best of all, he bounced and bounced and bounced, and he didn't bump into anything!

"But I already miss my old house," he said. "And I won't live next to little Roo anymore, and I'll miss him, too."

"I know you'll miss being neighbors with Kanga and Roo, but now you'll live much closer to me. We can have fun being neighbors—just like you and Roo did," Chrisopher Robin said reassuringly.

"Do you like to bounce?" Tigger asked.

"Sometimes," Christopher Robin said with a smile.

"Besides, dear, I promise to bring Roo over to visit just as often as you like," Kanga added.

"Well then, I hope everyone can stay a while," Tigger said. "We can play a game together and eat some cookies." Tigger opened his new pantry. But there were no cookies in sight!

He opened his new closet. There were no games, either!

"Kinda empty, isn't it?" Eeyore said.

"Yeah. Tiggers don't like empty houses. I like my old house better," Tigger said, crossing his arms.

Rabbit put his paws on his hips and stared at Tigger. "We aren't finished yet. We need to move all of your things from your old house to this house," he said.

"Everything?" Tigger asked.

"Every last little thing," Rabbit said. "That's a big job, so we'll start first thing tomorrow morning."

The friends all regrouped at Tigger's old house the next morning. As Rabbit instructed, everyone brought all the boxes they could find.

"Wow, boxes are fun!" Roo cried as he jumped in and out of empty boxes. "Look at me hiding!"

Tigger joined in on the fun, too!

"Stop bouncing, Tigger and Roo. There'll be time for fun later," Rabbit grumbled. "Right now, we've got to pack Tigger's things."

Tigger packed all his games and his stuffed animals in a box. He took out his favorite lion and hugged him tight. "I want you to stay with me," he said.

Rabbit carefully packed Tigger's dishes.

Kanga gently packed Tigger's clothes.

Pooh and Piglet packed up all of Tigger's food.

71

Soon Eeyore arrived with his donkey cart. "We can use this to haul your bigger things like furniture and whatnot," he said helpfully.

Christopher Robin and Owl hoisted Tigger's bed, table, and chairs onto the cart. Then Owl and Gopher loaded on the boxes that were done being packed. They secured everything with some string.

"Time to move it out!" Rabbit cried.

Eeyore pulled the big cart as everyone else pushed.

Soon they reached Tigger's new home. "Now my new home will be perfect!" Tigger exclaimed as they all unloaded the cart. His friends helped him carry everything inside.

"Thanks for your help, everyone," he said when they were done. "Moving was as easy as pie!"

After his friends had gone, Tigger put his toys on his new shelves. He pushed his bed under the back window, just where he wanted it. He set his table and chairs in the middle of the big kitchen. He put his cereal and other food in his new pantry.

When he was all finished, he sat down to rest. "Hmmm, this seems like an awfully quiet house," he said. He tried out a few bounces, but he quickly decided that he wasn't in such a bouncy mood after all.

"I sure miss Roo," he sighed.

Just then, Tigger heard a little voice call out his name. It was Roo! He and Kanga were at Tigger's door.

"Roo! Kanga! Come on in!" Tigger said.

"We've brought you a bag of cookies," Kanga said.

"Yummy!" Tigger cried.

Soon all of Tigger's friends were at his door. Everyone had brought a different gift for Tigger to celebrate his move into his new house.

"Now that Tigger is all settled in, I believe it's time for a little fun," Rabbit declared.

"Hooray!" Tigger exclaimed as he and his friends skipped, hopped, and happily bounced from room to room. "This is the kind of fun Tiggers love best!"

Pooh Welcomes Winter

"Winter will be here soon," Winnie the Pooh said one day to his best friend, Piglet. "That's what Christopher Robin says."

"Who's Winter?" Piglet asked.

"The someone who is coming soon," Pooh said.

"Oh, a visitor!" Piglet said. "We should do something nice for him."

"We could give him a party," Pooh suggested.

"That's a great idea!" Piglet agreed.

"Come on," said Pooh. "Let's go tell the others. We must start preparing right away! We don't know when exactly Winter will be coming, after all."

By the time the two friends got to Kanga's house, they were so chilled that they had to stay for tea. When they were finally warm enough to remember why they were there, Pooh turned to his friends. "Winter is coming soon, and we're going to throw him a party."

"Oh, boy! A party! Tiggers love parties!" Tigger cried excitedly.

"Let's go!" Roo cried.

As they opened the door, a pile of snow dropped from the roof and buried them. The wind was quiet. The Hundred-Acre Wood seemed to be napping under a blanket of white. Piglet, Pooh, Tigger, Roo, and Kanga were under a white blanket, too!

They blinked.

"How will we ever get to the party?" Piglet asked, buried up to his waist in snow. "The snow is so deep."

"Don't worry, little buddy. We'll go by sled," Tigger said.

Tigger and Pooh pulled Piglet and Roo on a sled while Kanga waved good-bye to them from the doorway. As they went, Roo reached over the side and grabbed snow to make snowballs. He piled them one by one on the sled.

"These will make good presents for Winter," he told Piglet.

"Winter has arrived," Owl declared as he passed by overhead. Swooping down, he perched himself on a branch to talk to the friends. "I heard Christopher Robin say so."

"Oh, do you know where Winter is?" Pooh said.

"I can't say I do," Owl admitted.

"We'll have to hurry and find him," Pooh said. He told Owl about the party. "Would you fly over and tell Rabbit and Gopher?"

"And Eeyore, too," Piglet added.

"I'd be happy to oblige," Owl said.

As Owl flew off, Tigger and Pooh climbed onto the sled with Piglet and Roo. They all shouted excitedly as they slid down the hill toward Christopher Robin's house. He would know where to find Winter!

When they reached the bottom of the hill, they could see a figure that looked like Christopher Robin up in the distance.

"Hello!" Pooh called.

But Christopher Robin didn't answer.

"Oh, no!" Piglet cried. "Maybe he's frozen in the cold!"

"That's not Christopher Robin. That's Winter!" Tigger cried.

"Winter?" Pooh whispered. "How do you know?"

"Tiggers always know Winter when they see him," Tigger replied. "That big white face—that carroty nose. Who else could he be?"

"He looks shy," Pooh pointed out. "We should be extra friendly." He walked right up to Winter. "How do you do?" he said, shaking Winter's stick hand. "I'm Pooh, and this is Piglet, Roo, and Tigger."

But Winter didn't answer.

Piglet nudged Pooh. "Tell him about the party."

"What party?" Pooh asked.

"His party!" Piglet replied.

"Oh, yes. We are so happy to have you in the Hundred-Acre Wood, so we are throwing a party in your honor," Pooh said.

Winter did not say anything.

"Oh, d-d-dear," Piglet stuttered. "He's frozen!"

"Quick! We better get him to the party and warm him up," Tigger cried. Together, the friends hoisted Winter onto their sled.

Roo showed him the snowballs. "I made these just for you."

But Winter did not even look down.

"Wow, he's in bad shape. We gotta hurry!" Tigger said.

Tigger and Pooh pulled while Roo and Piglet pushed. When they finally reached Pooh's house, the others were already there. Owl had hung a big friendly sign over Pooh's door that said WELCOME WINTUR.

Eeyore had stuck a pine branch in the snow. Little icicles sparkled on its needles. Rabbit and Gopher were inside making hot chocolate and honey carrot cake.

Pooh and Tigger wrested Winter off the sled. "Give him the comfy chair by the fire! Gopher, get him some hot chocolate," Rabbit ordered.

Everyone fussed over Winter. Still, he did not say a word. Next to the fire, his carrot nose drooped. His stick hands fell.

"Oh, my!" Piglet cried.

"Maybe he's not the party type," Eeyore said.

"What are we going to do?" Rabbit asked anxiously.

Just then, Christopher Robin came in. "Has anyone seen my snowman?" he asked.

"No, but maybe you can help us. We brought Winter here for a special party, but he doesn't seem to like it."

"Silly old bear," Christopher Robin said with a laugh. "Winter is not a who. It's a what! That's not winter—that's my snowman!"

"He's not Winter?" Pooh asked, confused.

"No. Winter is the season—you know, the time of year. Cold snow and mistletoe . . . warm fires and good friends."

"Now, come on," Christopher Robin said. "We'd better get the snowman back outside before he melts."

"Oh, d-d-dear," Piglet said. "I hope we haven't ruined him!"

"Snowmen are easy to fix," Christopher Robin said reassuringly. Together, the friends took the snowman outside. They undrooped his nose and stuck his stick hands back on.

"Well, so much for the party," Eeyore said sadly.

"We should still have a party to celebrate winter. That's a great idea!" Christopher Robin said.

Together, the friends threw Roo's snowballs. They took turns riding on Tigger's sled. They made snow angels. They danced around the snowman and sang songs.

Later, they took a break for honey carrot cake and hot chocolate. The friends all gathered around the fire. Christopher Robin gave Pooh a little hug. "Happy winter, Pooh," he said.

"Happy winter," Pooh replied.

Scavenger Hunt

Christopher Robin was sitting on a tree stump in the Hundred-Acre Wood. It was a beautiful late-summer afternoon, and he was waiting to say hello to his friends.

"Hello, Christopher Robin," Pooh said as he and the others arrived. "What shall we do on this very fine day?"

"Why don't you all go on a scavenger hunt?" Christopher Robin suggested.

"Tiggers love scavenger hunts!" Tigger yelled. Then he paused. "What is a scavenger hunt, exactly?" he asked, scratching his head in confusion. He looked at Pooh, Piglet, Roo, and Eeyore. But they all shook their heads, too.

"A scavenger hunt is a game of looking for things," Christopher Robin explained to his friends.

"What kinds of things?" Rabbit asked.

Christopher Robin thought for a moment. "Oh, let me think. Why don't you look for a small jar of honey, a purple flower, and a red leaf?"

Then he smiled and added, "I also want you to find the greatest thing in the whole world."

Pooh was confused. "Isn't honey the greatest thing in the whole world?" he asked.

"Honey is pretty sweet," Christopher Robin said. "But there is something even greater."

"Something even greater than honey?" Pooh said. "We must find it!"

The friends went to Pooh's house first to find a small jar of honey. His smallest jar was high up on a shelf. Pooh pointed it out to his friends. It was the perfect size for carrying on a scavenger hunt. Pooh looked around. "But how will we get it down?" he wondered aloud.

"Climb up on my shoulders," Tigger suggested.

Pooh did as Tigger suggested. He could reach the middle shelf and a big jar of honey, but not the smaller one!

"Rabbit, can you help, too?" Pooh asked.

"Of course," Rabbit replied.

Rabbit climbed on top of Pooh and stretched out his arm. "I can't quite reach it, either," Rabbit said.

Rabbit looked down at the smallest member of their group. "Roo, could you hop up here, please?"

"Sure!" Roo said. He bounced up onto Rabbit's back and managed to grab the small jar of honey. He dropped it down to Kanga, who caught it gently in her bag.

"We found our first scavenger hunt item!" Kanga said.

"Now we need a leaf and a flower," Pooh said as they walked out of his house to start searching for the next item. "Does anybody remember which should be red and which should be purple?"

No one could quite recall.

"Well, here's a red flower," Pooh said, bending down to pick a flower growing near his front door. "And it smells nice."

"Then it's perfect!" Kanga said. Everyone else agreed.

Roo looked around the base of a tree near Pooh's house. Kneeling down, he grabbed a big yellow leaf. "I found a leaf, but it's not purple!" he said excitedly, showing the others.

"I think I have some purple paint at my house," Rabbit said. "We can paint the leaf purple. Will it still count for our scavenger hunt?"

"I think so," Pooh said.

Together, they all headed to Rabbit's house. After pulling a half-filled can of paint from his closet, Rabbit delicately started painting the leaf. Everyone took a turn painting it. In no time, the leaf was a perfect grape-colored shade of purple!

After giving it a little time to dry, Kanga placed the leaf in her bag next to the small pot of honey and the red flower.

"Now all we need to do is find the greatest thing in the whole world," Piglet said.

"Where do you think we'll find it?" Roo asked.

"Maybe it's hiding somewhere in the woods," Tigger suggested.

"Let's search the Hundred-Acre Wood," Pooh said. "Together we might be able to find it!"

They headed back into the woods. "Greatest thing in the world, where are you?" Pooh called. Tigger searched under rocks. Rabbit checked in trees. Eeyore looked in the clearings. Owl checked the treetops. And Roo and Kanga looked near the streams. But the greatest thing in the world was nowhere to be found.

The friends searched and searched the Hundred-Acre Wood. They couldn't find the greatest thing in the world anywhere. Soon it grew quite late and dark. The friends decided to find Christopher Robin to show him how they had done on the scavenger hunt. They all held hands so no one would get lost in the dark.

Finally, after what seemed like forever, they found Christopher Robin sitting on the same tree stump, waiting for them. They had made it all the way back to where they had started.

"Have you finished the scavenger hunt?" Christopher Robin asked.

"No," Pooh said sadly. "But we all looked together."

"And we found almost everything," Tigger added.

Christopher Robin smiled. "Friends working together *is* the greatest thing in the whole world," he explained. "So you did find it after all."

The friends all hugged, glad they had spent a fantastic day completing the scavenger hunt—together.

A Good Night's Sleep

It was springtime in the Hundred-Acre Wood. Winnie the Pooh and Piglet were taking a walk in the warm sunshine.

"Hooray! The cold winter is over!" Piglet cheered.

"No more mittens and scarves," said Pooh.

"No more cold noses and toes," added Piglet.

"And plenty of yummy honey!" finished Pooh.

Pooh and Piglet walked until they reached their friend Rabbit's house.

Rabbit was outside working in his garden. He looked very tired and a little grumpy.

"What's the matter, Rabbit?" Piglet asked. "Aren't you happy that it's spring?"

"Don't even say the word! I hate spring!" Rabbit moaned.

Pooh and Piglet were puzzled, so Rabbit explained. "You see that bird family up there? They sing before the sun even comes up—right outside my bedroom window! I can't get any sleep!"

"Oh, dear," said Piglet. "We must do something."

Pooh wasn't sure what to say to Rabbit. "Perhaps it would help if you moved somewhere else?"

Rabbit jumped up with excitement. "Oh, Pooh! What a great idea! I would love to move in with you!"

Unfortunately for Pooh, that wasn't what he had meant at all! But now it looked like he would have an unexpected guest.

So Pooh and Piglet helped move a few of Rabbit's things to Pooh's house. As they were finishing up, the bird family flew away from Rabbit's tree.

"Look!" said Pooh. "The birds are flying away!"

"They'll be back soon—singing as usual," Rabbit told him. "They're just going out to get a bite to eat."

"Oh . . ." said Pooh, a little disappointed.

When the friends reached Pooh's home, they began unpacking.
"Rabbit," said Pooh, "you sure have brought a lot of things."
Suddenly, there seemed to be very little room for Pooh.

The next morning, Rabbit woke up early after a wonderful night of sleep.

"Rise and shine!" he called, pulling back Pooh's covers. Pooh immediately pulled them back up again. He was still sleepy!

"Pooh, it's time to get up!" scolded Rabbit. "The vegetables aren't going to plant themselves!"

Once Pooh had finally gotten out of bed, they walked to Rabbit's vegetable garden. Together, they planted seeds in neat little rows.

Perhaps bears aren't meant for such hard work, thought Pooh. But at least he could enjoy the cheerful songs of the bird family, who sang all day. Pooh rather liked their music.

Later, Piglet arrived.

"I was just over at your house, Pooh," said Piglet. "But you weren't home."

"No, I'm not home," Pooh said sadly.

Pooh took Piglet aside. "I am rather tired because Rabbit woke me up," said Pooh. "And I've got an awful rumbly in my tumbly. You see, I haven't had any honey."

Pooh wished that he could have his little house all to himself again.

"Maybe Owl will know what to do," suggested Piglet.

When Pooh and Piglet found Owl, he was too busy to help.

"I'm afraid I simply can't talk right now," Owl said. "My favorite napping branch is waiting for me." Owl flew up to an old oak tree. But a little sparrow was sitting right in Owl's favorite spot!

"It looks like my branch is already occupied!" said Owl. "I guess I'll just have to find another one!"

As Owl flew off, Pooh began to have an idea. He and Piglet hurried to Pooh's Thoughtful Spot to come up with a plan.

"We need the bird family to find a different branch to sing on," Pooh said.

"But how will we get them to move?" asked Piglet.

Pooh sat for a bit. "Think, think, think," he said as he patted his head. Finally, all his thinking turned into a real plan.

"When the birds fly off at night to look for food, we will take their spot," said Pooh. "Then they will have to find another favorite branch."

"Just like Owl and the sparrow!" Piglet cheered.

Pooh told Rabbit about their plan to move the bird family. Now Rabbit would be able stay in his own home without worrying about the birds' morning songs.

"What a splendid idea," Rabbit said. "I'm glad I thought of it!"

They moved all of Rabbit's things back into his house.

That night, Pooh and Piglet waited by the tree until the birds flew off. When they did, the friends started to climb up to the birds' favorite branch.

Rabbit offered to sit out there with them, but there was only room for two.

"At least take this blanket," said Rabbit. "And thank you for your help, dear friends."

So Pooh and Piglet waited. And waited. And waited. They tried their best to stay awake, but the blanket was awfully warm and comfortable. Soon the friends were fast asleep. The next morning, Pooh and Piglet woke up to the sound of singing birds. "Look!" Pooh said, pointing to the sky.

The bird family swooped down toward their favorite branch. But when they saw that there wasn't any room on their branch, they flew in a different direction.

"Hooray!" said Piglet. "The plan worked!"

The pair checked to see if Rabbit was asleep.

"He won't be woken up by singing birds today," said Piglet. Pooh and Piglet walked toward their homes as the sun rose over the Hundred-Acre Wood.

"I'm sure the bird family has found another favorite branch by now," said Pooh.

Pooh was right. The birds had found a new branch—right outside his window! It seemed he would have to get used to a few more unexpected guests.

Luckily, Pooh didn't mind the birds' song. He thought it sounded a bit like a lullaby. Within minutes, Pooh was once again fast asleep.

At last, Rabbit, Pooh, and the bird family were all happy with their homes.

Rabbit's Bad Mood

One spring morning, Rabbit entered his garden and found a horrible surprise. His carrots had shrunk, the lettuce had wilted, and the turnips hadn't grown. Only the radishes looked edible.

He knelt down to pull a radish from the dirt. "This is a disaster!" he cried as he took a bite. "This radish is too small! And it tastes terrible! I cannot eat that!" He pulled out another one—same thing. Another one—but it was even smaller than the first. Rabbit pulled them all out, but they were all too small and too bitter to eat!

Disappointed, he turned to his carrots. One by one, he pulled each shriveled-up carrot out of the ground and threw it as far as he could.

Looking around his garden, Rabbit felt his bad mood sink in.

"This is the worst day ever!" he said as he jumped up and down on the spot where the turnips should have grown.

Just then, he spotted Tigger bouncing over to him.

"Hello, Rabbit!" Tigger said happily. "I didn't know you could bounce so well. Will you come and bounce with me?"

"Tigger, I don't think this is the right time to be so happy," Rabbit replied.

"Okay. I'll go now," Tigger said as he bounced away.

"Perfect," Rabbit said. "Now I'm on my own. Alone with these lettuce heads that are only good to be . . . stepped on!" he concluded as he trampled them.

There was not much left of Rabbit's garden when Piglet arrived. He had thought that Rabbit would be happy to see him, but now he was not so sure.

"G-g-good m-morning, Rabbit," he stuttered.

"What's so good about it?" Rabbit snapped. "What do you want? Can't you see I'm in a bad mood?"

"I don't see anything. But, oh, look at your garden! The carrots and lettuce have been pulled out!"

"I think you'd better go, Piglet," said Rabbit. "This bad mood hanging over me is only getting larger!"

Piglet looked nervously over Rabbit's head. Piglet didn't see anything, but he thought perhaps he was too small to see such a big bad mood. Piglet started to shiver and shake. If Rabbit's bad mood came closer, it would gobble him up!

"Bye, Rabbit!" Piglet called as he ran back down the road.

Piglet ran straight to Pooh's house to tell him what was going on.

"I understand," said Pooh as he scratched his head. "Rabbit is not happy to be in a bad mood."

"Exactly!" said Piglet. He was relieved that Pooh understood so well.

"You say it is above Rabbit, but you can't see it?" Pooh asked, deep in thought.

"Yes," Piglet confirmed.

"Then I think the bad mood is a sort of cloud that prevents Rabbits from being happy," Pooh concluded.

"Or maybe it's like a storm inside his head," suggested Piglet. "I think I saw lightning come out of Rabbit's eyes."

"Maybe," Pooh agreed.

The two friends went to Owl's to ask for his opinion. Piglet told the whole story, including the invisible cloud and lightning. When he was done, Owl thought for a moment.

"If Rabbit is in a bad mood and he doesn't want to be in a bad mood," Owl reasoned, "then the bad mood must be removed from him."

"By dousing the lightning in his eyes with water?" Piglet asked.

"By blowing away the invisible cloud?" suggested Pooh.

"I think," Owl said, "that we should try to understand *why* Rabbit is in a bad mood. If we understand why, then maybe Rabbit's bad mood will go away by itself."

The three friends were headed toward Rabbit's when Tigger joined them. He wanted to know more about Rabbit's bad mood, too.

As the friends approached Rabbit's house, they could see him kicking the cabbage in his garden. They hoped that they could help their friend improve his mood!

"Why are you in a bad mood, Rabbit?" Owl asked when they reached the garden.

Rabbit gestured wildly to his devastated garden. "Shrunken carrots," he bellowed. "Wilted lettuce, inedible radishes, and not a puny turnip in sight!"

"Is it possible that you could have forgotten to water your plants?" Owl asked.

Rabbit clutched the handle of his shovel. Piglet was *sure* he saw streaks of lightning flashing in his eyes.

"Are you suggesting that I did not do my job properly?" Rabbit yelled.

Spreading his wings, Owl turned to his friends. "Now *here* is what I call being in a bad mood."

"Yes, I am in a bad mood!" Rabbit cried. "I won't have enough food for winter, and you're calling me a bad gardener. Me! When I live only for my work!"

"That's not what I meant," Owl said. "We all know you are an excellent gardener!"

"Maybe worms are eating Rabbit's seeds," suggested Piglet.

"Impossible. Our friend Gopher ate the worms last spring," Rabbit grumbled.

"Maybe the turnip seeds are still in your cellar without you realizing it," Tigger suggested.

"Maybe," Rabbit said. He wasn't 100 percent sure that he'd actually planted the seeds.

"Maybe it was the bad weather," added Pooh. "It rained an awful lot this year."

"So much that I almost drowned in a deep puddle," Piglet added.

"And I missed the beautifullest bounce when I landed in the mud!" Tigger cried.

"No plant can grow in such conditions," confirmed Owl.

"So that must be what happened," Rabbit said.

"Rabbit, we are going to help you plant your garden all over again," Pooh declared. "It's only June. Your vegetables will have plenty of time to grow before winter!"

All the rest of the friends agreed. They quickly got to work helping Rabbit replant his garden. Even Eeyore joined in!

As the afternoon wore on, the friends had lots of fun removing the bad crops and working together to plant new seeds. Rabbit felt his bad mood lifting. He was grateful to have such a great group of friends!

Why Take a Nap?

On a sunny summer afternoon, all the friends of the Hundred-Acre Wood were gathered around Tigger. He was explaining how Tigger stripes were different from bee stripes. Suddenly, Kanga called for Roo. It was time for his nap. "Roo! Are you coming inside?"

Roo shook his head. "I'm listening to what Tigger has to say. It is very interesting."

"Hoo-hoo-hoo!" Tigger was saying. "I'm telling you, bees don't need stripes to fly. Less weight, more lightness! They should take them off!"

"Roo!" Kanga insisted.

"Are you sure it's time?" Roo grumbled.

"Same as yesterday, darling," Kanga said.

"What if I took a nap tonight, after dinner, when I go to bed? I will sleep very tight to catch up. Like this." Roo shut his eyes and made a funny face.

"Oh! Oh! Oh!" Tigger shouted. "Let me show you how to take a nap. Watch me!"

He threw his paws in the air, twisted his tail, and sailed through the window into Roo's bedroom. He landed on Roo's bed.

"I still don't understand why I should take a nap now," argued Roo. "I am not tired, and I want to keep playing."

"Well, I could do with a little nap," commented Eyore. "But I don't mind if I can't sleep. I'm used to being tired."

"But I don't want to take a nap," Roo said.

"Hello!" called Tigger as he came back outside. "Here I am! Look how bouncy I feel after a nap!"

Roo shook his head and pointed to the sky. "Nobody sleeps during the day! The sun doesn't sleep, the sky doesn't sleep, the flowers don't, and the bees don't. . . ."

Owl cleared his throat before he spoke. "Like my grandfather used to say, owls sleep during daytime. It is important to sleep in the daytime, dear Roo."

"You know," added Pooh, "sometimes after looking for a honey tree, I am so tired that I forget to take a nap. But when I remember, I recall that a good nap is really nice."

"Then why don't you all go and take naps?" Roo said. "Why am I the only one who has to sleep while everyone else plays?"

"Play!" Rabbit cried, horrified. "But I have to work!"

"So do I," Tigger insisted.

"You!" Rabbit laughed. "Tigger, you don't even know the meaning of that word! After summer comes fall. Winter is getting close! We will have to gather wood and repair windows. What am I doing here wasting my time? There are so many important things to do!"

As Rabbit walked away, everyone remembered the important things they had to do.

"I must count my honey pots to make sure I have enough for winter," Poo said. "If only my pots could count themselves!"

"And I need to count my books to see if I need to write more," Owl announced.

"Oh, dear," Piglet said. "I must have quite a bit of work, but I'm not sure what it is! What about you, Tigger?"

"Who, me?" Tigger replied. "Working is what Tiggers do best." Tigger picked up Roo and sent him flying like a ball into his mother's arms.

"If you asked me, which no one did, of course," added Eyore, "I would reply that I have to build my house again, since Tigger knocked it down."

"Have a good nap, little Roo!" Pooh called as the friends all hurried to do their work.

Inside, Kanga put Roo to bed. His little head sank into the soft pillow.

"Sweet dreams, darling!" Kanga whispered.

She had barely closed the door when Roo jumped out of bed.

He went to his toy chest. There, he picked some toys—a teddy bear, a stuffed caterpillar, and a puppet.

151

Roo placed them in his bed.

"Now it's time for you to nap," he declared to the toys. "Go to sleep!"

He sat on his bed next to his toys to watch them. But they would not fall asleep.

"There is only one way to get them to nap," Roo said. "I'll lie down next to them and pretend that I am sleeping."

When Kanga came back a short while later, Roo did not hear the door open. He and his toys were fast asleep.

Two hours later, Roo woke up from his nap. He felt great. Kanga had a delicious snack prepared for him—a bowl of hot chocolate, toast with honey, and orange juice.

"It's like having breakfast again!" Roo exclaimed happily.

When he was finished with his snack, Roo went outside to look for his friends.

Roo's friends were all done with their work. Even Rabbit was finished.

So Roo decided to organize a big sack race. Piglet and Roo stood in one big canvas bag, and Pooh and Tigger stood in another. The last one barely contained Eyore.

"Well, I am a bit bulky," he mumbled to himself.

On Owl's signal, the teams moved forward as fast as they could. Rabbit sat on the sidelines, wondering why just watching was making him tired.

Roo and Piglet won the race.

"Wow!" Roo cried. "That was so fun!"

"All that racing makes my stomach hurt," Piglet whined.

"I can't bounce with this sack," Tigger said as he tried to catch his breath. "That's not fair!"

"Let's race again!" Roo exclaimed.

But none of Roo's friends were ready to get back on their feet! The competitors were too tired to start another race.

Roo smiled at his friends. "Next time, you should take a nap!"

Boo to You, Winnie the Pooh

Once each year, there comes a most peculiar day. The dark grows darker. The leaves rattle on the trees. And everything is a tad spookier.

On this particular day, Winnie the Pooh was dressed like a bee, snacking on his last drop of honey.

"Oh, Halloween," he chuckled. "Though I'm not fond of tricking, I do enjoy treating."

A few minutes later, a skeleton bounced in.

"Not late, am I?" asked Tigger, for that was who the bouncer was. Behind him were two Eeyores—the real one, who was wrapped in bandages like a mummy, and Gopher, who had dressed up like Eeyore.

"Hello, Eeyore and Gopher," said Pooh.

"Dagnabbit!" said Gopher. "You know it's *me*?" He left to find a new costume.

"C'mon, Pooh!" cried Tigger. "We'd better get a move on!"

"But first we need to get Piglet," Pooh replied.

Piglet was putting the finishing touches on his costume when he heard a Tigger-like "Boo-hoo-hoo!" coming from his entryway.

"Why, Piglet," said Pooh as his friend hurried to greet them, "where's your costume?"

"We've got to get Halloweenin'!" said Tigger.

"Oh . . . u-uh . . ." Piglet stammered. He didn't really want to go outside.

"While Piglet gets ready," said Pooh, "I'll try out my costume on our friends at the honey tree."

"But Pooh—" Piglet said, following his friend.

"Perhaps it would be best," Pooh said as he started out the door, "if you didn't say my name. It might make the bees suspicious."

But the bees knew exactly what Pooh was trying to do! They began to buzz angrily.

Pooh and the others ran away from the honey tree as fast as they could.

Nearby, Rabbit inspected his pumpkin patch.

"Perfect!" he proclaimed.

Bzzzzzzzzzzz! Suddenly, Rabbit heard the bees. He looked up just in time to see Pooh, Piglet, Tigger, and Eeyore smash into his beautiful pumpkins. The bees flew away, disturbed by all the chaos.

"Of all my favorite holidays," Rabbit sighed, "Halloween isn't one!"

Soon it grew dark, and Piglet hurried home. As he got into his costume, he realized he was just too scared to go outside.

Suddenly, there was a knock at the door.

"Who . . . who's there?" he squeaked.

"It's me . . . them . . . us!" said a Pooh-sounding voice.

"Pooh Bear?" asked Piglet. "How can I be certain it's you? Perhaps if you said something only you would say, then I'd be certain. How about 'I am Pooh'?"

"You are?" said a confused Pooh. "Then who am I?"

"It *is* you!" squealed Piglet, jumping out of his costume and opening the door.

"Piglet," said Pooh, "will you be joining us for Halloween?"

"I'm afraid I'm just too afraid," Piglet replied.

"That's okay," said Pooh Bear. "We won't have a Halloween. We'll have a Hallo*wasn't*."

"Thank you, Pooh Bear," Piglet said, smiling.

Piglet and Pooh explained their plan to Eeyore and Tigger, and with that, everyone went home.

Alone once more, Piglet created lots of notes telling all the spookables and monstery beasts to stay away. They had to know that it was a Hallo*wasn't* at his house somehow!

165

Soon a storm began to rage outside. Pooh looked out his window. "I hope Piglet isn't too frightened," he said. "I suspect that something should be done. But what?"

He tried to concentrate. "Think, think, think!" he muttered. And, to no one's greater surprise than his own, he did just that!

"Just because Piglet can't have Halloween with us," said Pooh, "there's no reason why we can't have Hallo*wasn't* with him!"

A little while later, Tigger was bouncing around when two figures opened his door.

"*Spookables!*" hollered Tigger, tripping over his tail.

The spookables removed their sheets. It was Pooh and Eeyore.

"We're on our way to Piglet's to have a Hallo*wasn't*," said Pooh. "Would you care to come? We made new costumes since the other ones were torn in the pumpkin patch."

"What are we standin' around here for?" Tigger said, snatching a sheet.

They'd almost reached Piglet's house when a tree branch snagged Pooh's bedsheet. Pooh was certain he'd been clutched by the claw of a spookable!

"Help!" shouted Pooh.

"Pooh Bear?" Piglet said, hearing Pooh's cries coming from just outside his house.

Tigger and Eeyore, still wrapped in their ghostly bedsheets, tried to free Pooh from the branch.

"Oh, no!" Piglet cried when he saw them. "Spookables got Pooh! I must help him, Halloween or no Halloween!"

Suddenly, Piglet remembered the costume he'd made.

"I'll save you, Pooh!" he cried, putting it on.

He stumbled outside and yelled, "Boo!" as loud as he could.

Pooh, Eeyore, and Tigger looked up in horror and ran away, leaving Pooh's costume on the branch.

They ran past a startled Gopher, who was now wearing a Rabbit costume.

"Look out! Spookables!" they shouted.

Gopher looked up just as Piglet ran into him. They both went rolling after the others.

Rabbit, who had been trying to keep his remaining pumpkins dry with an umbrella, glanced up. "Not again!" he cried, just before Pooh, Tigger, Eeyore, Piglet, and Gopher collided with him.

Costumes and pumpkin pieces flew everywhere.

Finally, the friends untangled themselves and discovered there was not a single spookable around.

"You saved us," Pooh told Piglet. "You're here and the spookables aren't. You must have chased them away."

"Way to go, Piglet!" exclaimed Tigger.

Piglet's friends shook his hand. "Wait half a second, Piglet," said Tigger. "You aren't dressed up as anything for Halloween!"

Piglet realized he'd lost his costume in all the excitement. Then he smiled. "Oh, but I am," he said. "I've decided to be Pooh's best and bravest friend!"

"And that," said Pooh, smiling down at Piglet, "is precisely who you are."

Piglet's Night-Lights

It was twilight in the Hundred-Acre Wood when Winnie the Pooh knocked on Piglet's door.

Piglet opened the door and looked around anxiously. "Are you really quite sure about this, Pooh?" he asked. "It's getting awfully dark out there, and it's so light and cozy in here. Maybe we could just camp out in my living room."

"That would be a camp IN, not a campout," Pooh said. He reminded Piglet that their friends would be going, too.

Pooh helped Piglet get ready. He stuffed haycorn muffins into Piglet's backpack while Piglet packed his favorite blanket and teddy bear.

"I have the feeling I'm forgetting something," Piglet said.

"Well, let's see," Pooh said. "We have honey." He patted the sticky honey pot in his pack.

"And we have plenty of muffins. What else could we possibly need for our campout?"

As Pooh and Piglet walked toward the campsite, it got darker and darker. Piglet got more and more frightened. "What's that?" he said, pointing to a scary-looking shape in the trees.

"I'm not certain, Piglet," Pooh said nervously. "Maybe if we close our eyes, it will go away." He and Piglet shut their eyes and stood very still.

"Hello down there!" called a voice from above.

Pooh and Piglet both jumped, startled. All they could see were two eyes.

"Why, it's only me—Owl," the voice said. "I thought you two might need help finding the others."

"Oh, thank you, Owl!" Piglet said.

When the friends reached the campsite, it was completely dark. Pooh bumped into Rabbit, who was struggling to put up the tent.

"Well, don't just stand there," Rabbit said. "I need all the help I can get!"

"Did I hear someone say 'help'?" Tigger called, bouncing into the clearing. "Have no fear, Tigger's here—with illuminagination!" he said proudly, holding up a lantern.

"Oh, and you brought a light, too!" cried Piglet, peeking out from under the hood of his jacket. "Thank goodness—it's awfully dark out here."

While the friends got to work setting up the tent, Piglet began to unpack. "Oh, no!" he wailed. "I forgot my night-light! I can't sleep without one." He wrung his hands. "What am I going to do?"

"Don't worry, Buddy Boy," Tigger said. "You can use my lantern as a night-light!" Just then, the lantern flickered out.

"On second thought," Tigger said, digging through Rabbit's bag, "Long Ears must have something in here you can use."

Tigger pulled out a kite, a flowerpot, and kitchen pans. Finally, he spotted a flashlight. Tigger tried to turn it on, but nothing happened.

At that moment, there was a crash in the nearby bushes. "Look who we found!" Pooh exclaimed. He pointed to Eeyore, who was standing next to Rabbit and Owl.

Eeyore looked around. "Can't have a campout without a campfire," he said.

Everyone agreed. They gathered some sticks, and soon a fire was burning.

"Campfires certainly are pleasant," Piglet said.

"They do a fantalicious job cooking marshy-mallows, too!" Tigger cried, wrestling with a particularly gooey marshmallow.

"Fire is fine," Rabbit said. "But I think sunlight is the best light of all—it makes my vegetables grow."

"I like the way the sun warms my tummy when I lie in the grass," Pooh said.

"And the colors at sunset are splendid," Piglet added.

"Look at that shadow on the tent!" Tigger interrupted.

"That looks like your tail to me," Rabbit said with a smile.

"Well, what do you know!" Tigger replied.

"Guess what this is," Rabbit said, fluttering his hands like a butterfly.

Tigger and Owl looked at the tent. A shape was moving on it. "Why, it's a shadow puppet!" Owl declared.

The friends played with shadow puppets until bedtime. Then almost everyone went to bed. Piglet wouldn't leave the light of the fire, though. Pooh decided to keep him company.

After a short while, the fire began to fade. "Maybe we should go to sleep now, Piglet," Pooh said, yawning.

"I can't sleep without a night-light, Pooh," Piglet replied.

Pooh tapped his forehead to wake up any ideas that might be there. "Think, think, think," he said.

Looking up at the night sky, Pooh thought of something. "The stars are night-lights, Piglet," he said, pointing up at the sparkling stars.

Just then, a firefly landed right between Pooh's eyes. Crossing his eyes to see it, Pooh tumbled off the log he was sitting on. "And so are the fireflies," he added.

Piglet looked around. "There are night-lights everywhere!" he cried. He pointed to the moon. "Look how bright the moon is tonight," he said. "It's even brighter than my own night-light. I feel much better."

"Do you think you might be able to sleep now, Piglet?" Pooh asked his friend with a huge yawn. "Piglet?"

But Piglet didn't answer. He was already fast asleep!